A Break-of-Day Book

Ever since 1928, when Wanda Gág's classic *Millions of Cats* appeared, Coward-McCann has been publishing books of high quality for young readers. Among them are the easy-to-read stories known as Break-of-Day books. This series appears under the colophon shown above — a rooster crowing in the sunrise — which is adapted from one of Wanda Gág's illustrations for *Tales from Grimm*.

Though the language used in Break-of-Day books is deliberately kept as clear and as simple as possible, the stories are not written in a controlled vocabulary. And while chosen to be within the grasp of readers in the primary grades, their content is far-ranging and varied enough to captivate children who have just begun crossing the momentous threshold into the world of books.

Weekly Reader Books presents

Nate the Great

and the

FISHY PRIZE

by Marjorie Weinman Sharmat

illustrations by Marc Simont

Coward-McCann Inc. New York

Text copyright © 1985 by Marjorie Weinman Sharmat
Illustrations copyright © 1985 by Marc Simont

Printed in the United States of America

Library of Congress Cataloging in Publication Data
Sharmat, Marjorie Weinman.
Nate the great and the fishy prize.
Summary: Though it means Nate can't get his
dog ready for the smartest pet contest, he agrees
to search for the missing prize for the contest.
1. Children's stories, American. [1. Mystery and
detective stories] I. Simont, Marc, ill. II. Title.
PZ7.S5299Natm   1985   [E]   84-15545
ISBN:0-698-30745-3

for my father Nathan "Nate" Weinman
who inspired this series,
and who was in every way
Nate the Great

I, Nate the Great,

am a detective.

I solve important cases.

I do important things.

This morning I was doing something

very important.

I was at the supermarket

buying dog shampoo

for my dog, Sludge.

Today Sludge was going to be

in a contest in the park

to choose the smartest pet

in the neighborhood.

I, Nate the Great, knew that

Sludge was the smartest.

And the dirtiest.

I wanted Sludge to be a clean winner.
I bought dog shampoo,
and flour, eggs, butter, milk,
salt, sugar and baking powder
to make pancakes.
I like pancakes.
I bought so many things
that the grocery bag bulged open.
I put the bag in the basket
on the back of my new bicycle
and started to ride home.

I rode past Rosamond's house.

Strange noises

were coming from inside her house.

I wondered what was happening.

But I kept my eyes straight ahead

to see where I was going.

Besides, strange noises

were the right kind of noises

to come from Rosamond's house.

Because Rosamond is strange.

When I got home,

Sludge was waiting for me.

"I bought you some shampoo,"
I said.

Sludge did not think
that was good news.

Sludge hates baths.

I put the grocery bag on the floor.

Before I could unpack it,

the telephone rang.

Rosamond was calling me.
She said, "I am in charge
of making the prize
for the Smartest Pet Contest."
"I know that," I said.
I, Nate the Great,
hated to think
what the prize would be.
"Well, I made the prize,
but it disappeared," Rosamond said.
"What was it?" I asked.
"It was an empty tuna fish can
with the word SMARTEST
hand-painted on it
in big gold letters,"
Rosamond said.

"Any pet would love to have it.

But now it's gone."

"You will have to make

another prize," I said.

"It's too late," Rosamond said.

"The contest starts in an hour.

Will you look for the tuna fish can?"

"I have to get Sludge ready

for the contest," I said.

"But there won't be a contest
unless you find the prize,"
Rosamond said.
I looked at Sludge.
He looked smart.
There had to be a contest.
"I, Nate the Great,
will take your case," I said.
"Sludge and I
will be right over."
I hung up.
I said to Sludge,
"We must look for a tuna fish can.
There is no time
to give you a bath."

Sludge thought

that was good news.

I wrote a quick note to my mother.

Sludge and I rushed to Rosamond's house.

There was no time to say hello.

"Show me where the prize was,"

I said.

Rosamond took me to her room.

It smelled fishy.

And there were things knocked over.

And things upside down.

And things all over the floor.

It was a mess.

"What happened?" I asked.

"Everyone came with their pets

to sign up for the contest,"

Rosamond said.

"Annie came with Fang.

Pip came with his parrot.

Finley came with his rat.

Oliver came with his favorite eel.

Claude came with a pig.

And Esmeralda came by herself.

She doesn't have any pets,

so she is going to be the judge.

Well, Fang ran after Claude's pig.

The pig ran after my four cats.

My cats ran after the rat.

Pip's parrot got all excited

and flew around and around.

Even Oliver's eel got excited.

They barked and squawked

and oinked and all sorts of things,

and they messed up my whole room."

"Yes, I, Nate the Great,

heard all the strange noises

when I rode by on my bicycle.

17

But where was the tuna fish can

when all of this was going on?"

"I had opened the window

and put the can on the sill

so the gold paint could dry

in the air," Rosamond said.

"When did you notice

that the can was gone?" I asked.

"Right after the stampede," Rosamond said.

"Everyone left,

and I started to clean up the room.

That's when I saw

that the prize was gone.

I looked all over the room for it."

"I will look again," I said.
"It could be somewhere in this mess.
It must have been knocked off
the windowsill.
Then perhaps one of those pets
who's supposed to be so smart
pushed or pulled
or dragged or kicked it."
"My cats are smart," Rosamond said.
"They are all going to win first prize."
Rosamond's cats could win first prize
for being strange.
I, Nate the Great, looked around the room.

"Did you paint the can in this room?"
I asked.

"No," Rosamond said.

"Good. I am looking for smudges
of gold paint. They might be a clue
to where the can went.
But if you had painted in this room,
you could have left smudges."

"I don't smudge," Rosamond said.

I, Nate the Great, went to the windowsill.

If I could find smudges of gold paint

inside the sill

or *outside* the sill,

I would know whether the can

went inside or outside.

But the can

had not left any clues behind.

Sludge was sniffing. And sniffing.

I asked Rosamond,

"Did you wash the tuna fish can

before you made it into a prize?"

"Sort of," Rosamond said.

"Sort of?" I said.

"How do you sort of wash

a tuna fish can?"

"My cats licked it," Rosamond said.

"They do a good job.

They love tuna fish."

"But they don't use soap," I said.

"That means the prize

may still smell fishy.

That is a clue."

I turned to Sludge.

"Fishy smell," I said.

Sludge and I could not find

the can in Rosamond's room.

"The can is not here," I said.

"Perhaps it went *out* the window."

Sludge and I rushed outside.

We looked around.

There was no tuna fish can.

There were no smudges of gold paint.

There was nothing but a sidewalk.

We walked back and forth.

Perhaps the can had been

pushed or pulled

or dragged or kicked up the street

or down the street.

But we could not find anything.

We went back inside.

"This is a very fishy case,"

I said to Rosamond.

"The can was on the windowsill.

So it had to be knocked

inside the house

or outside the house.

But it isn't inside and it isn't outside."

"Maybe someone took the can on purpose,"

Rosamond said.

I, Nate the Great, did not want

to tell Rosamond that no one

would take her tuna fish can on purpose.

That it was the dumbest prize

for the Smartest contest.

"I will have to speak to everyone

who was in this room," I said.

"Perhaps someone saw what happened

to the tuna fish can."

Sludge and I rushed to Claude's house.

Claude was there with a pig.

Claude is always losing things.

I was glad

he had not lost the pig.

Claude was brushing the pig's bristles

while she ate a big pile of food.

"I am getting Anastasia ready
for the Smartest Pet Contest," Claude said.
Anastasia oinked.
I watched her eat.
The food was disappearing fast.
I was thinking.. . .

The tuna fish can had completely disappeared.

Maybe it had disappeared *inside* something.

One way to make something disappear

is to eat it.

I, Nate the Great, spoke up.

"Pigs are supposed to eat like pigs.

Would Anastasia eat a tin can?"

"I don't know," Claude said.

"She's not my pig. She lives on a farm,

and I borrowed her for the contest.

But I keep losing her.

She finds her way back to me.

She's smart. That's why

she is going to win the contest."

Anastasia oinked again.

"May I open Anastasia's mouth?"

I asked.

"If you really want to," Claude said.

I, Nate the Great, did not really

want to open Anastasia's mouth.

But I had a case to solve.

I had a job to do.

Slowly I opened her mouth.

Quickly I closed her mouth.

"Anastasia did not eat

the tuna fish can," I said.

"How do you know?" Claude asked.

"Because the gold paint on the can

was wet. Anastasia would have

a gold mouth if she ate the can.

Tell me, did you see the can

on Rosamond's windowsill?"

"I saw it and I didn't see it,"

Claude said.

"That is an interesting answer,"
I said. "I, Nate the Great, say
that is an interesting answer."

"Well, I saw the can on the windowsill
just before everyone started to run around,"
Claude said.

"When it was all over,
I didn't see the can anymore."

"That is an old clue," I said.

"I already know that the can disappeared
during the animal stampede.
I, Nate the Great, need a new clue.
And I need it fast."
Sludge and I left.
I was sorry I had seen Anastasia.
She made me feel very hungry.
I wished I had time to go home
and make pancakes with the things
I had bought at the supermarket.
But I hadn't even had time
to unpack them.
And I knew there was not enough time left

to talk to everyone else

who had been in Rosamond's room.

Annie, Oliver, Pip,

Finley and Esmeralda were left.

I decided to go to Esmeralda's house.

I had two reasons.

Esmeralda is smart.

Esmeralda does not have a pet.

Perhaps she had a chance to see something

when everyone was busy

with their pets.

Esmeralda was sitting quietly

outside on her steps.

She did not have anybody
to wash or brush or feed or brag about.
I said, "I am looking for the tuna fish can
that was on Rosamond's windowsill.
Did you see it?"
"Yes," Esmeralda said. "I saw it
before everything went wild.
Fang was standing under it."

"Fang?" I said. "Tell me,

which way was he facing?"

"He was standing with his right side

next to the window," Esmeralda said.

"His fangs were showing,

and his tail

was swooshing back and forth."

I, Nate the Great, was thinking.

This was a new clue.

But did it mean anything?

Suddenly I knew that it was important.

Sludge and I

rushed to Annie's house.

She was giving Fang a bath.

He was sitting in the bathtub

all soapy and foamy.

And fangy.

"I am getting Fang ready for the contest,"
Annie said. "Everyone knows he is pretty.
Now they will find out he is smart."

I, Nate the Great,

already knew more about Fang

than I wanted to know.

Annie started to scrub Fang's tail.

"Stop!" I yelled.

"Fang may be wearing a clue."

"Fang isn't wearing anything,"

Annie said.

I, Nate the Great, got close to Fang.

I did not want to do that.

But I had to see his tail.

I was glad the clue

was on that end of him.

I leaned over.

I saw what I had hoped I would see.

Gold paint on Fang's tail.

It was on the right side.

"Happy Bath," I said to Fang.

Sludge and I

rushed back to Rosamond's house.

"I, Nate the Great, say

the tuna fish can

was knocked outside."

"How do you know that?" Rosamond asked.

"Because Fang was standing

with his right side next to the window," I said

"His tail was going back and forth.

He got gold paint on the right side

of his tail. That means his tail

hit the can going outward.

Right out the window.

Sludge and I

are going to look very hard

outside your house again."

"The contest is supposed to start
in fifteen minutes," Rosamond said.
"Then we will look very hard
and very fast," I said.
Sludge and I rushed outside.
We looked around again.
We walked up and down the sidewalk again.
It was a boring sidewalk.
Cracks, but no clues.

I, Nate the Great, was stumped.

This was definitely a tough, fishy case.

I was not going to solve it on time.

I was not going to solve it at all.

Sludge and I walked home.

We went into the kitchen.

Sludge sniffed the grocery bag.

Why was he sniffing the grocery bag?

It only had dog shampoo

and things for making pancakes,

and Sludge does not like dog shampoo

or pancakes.

But I could not think about the bag.

I had to think about the case.

I thought about the can

being knocked to the outside.

I thought about it happening

while everything was noisy and wild.

I thought about fishy smells

and things disappearing inside

Anastasia's stomach,

and gold paint.

I thought about Fang's tail.

Fang had taken home some gold paint
on his tail.
He did not know he had taken it home.
Annie did not know he had taken it home.
Perhaps someone had taken
the tuna fish can home,
but did not know it.
But how? Tuna fish cans do not stick to tails.
You can see a tuna fish can.
Unless . . . you can't see it!
Unless it is hidden from sight.
Unless it disappears into something
as big and bulgy
as Anastasia's stomach.
Suddenly I, Nate the Great, knew
I had solved the case.

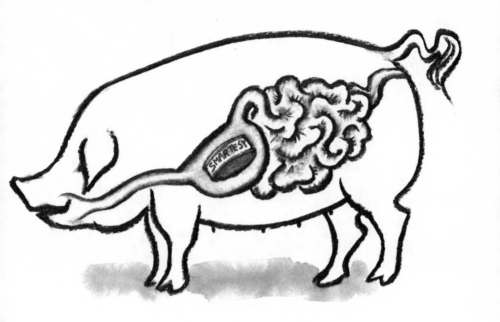

But I knew Sludge had solved it sooner.

He was still sniffing my grocery bag.

I looked inside the bag.

Then I put my hand inside the bag,

and pulled out an empty tuna fish can

with SMARTEST painted on it

in smudged gold letters.

I, Nate the Great, had taken the can!

And I knew how it had happened.

Fang knocked the can out the window

just as I was riding past Rosamond's house.

The can fell into the open grocery bag

that was in the basket

on the back of my bicycle.

I had taken the can home

without knowing it.

And now I must take the can to the contest.

Sludge and I rushed to the park,

where everyone was waiting

for the contest to start.

Rosamond was there with her four cats.

Annie was there with Fang.

Pip was there with his parrot.

Finley was there with his rat.

Oliver was there with his favorite eel.

Esmeralda was there with herself.

Claude and Anastasia were not there.

I was not surprised.

Either Claude had lost Anastasia

or Anastasia had lost Claude.

I held up the prize.

I said, "This was in my grocery bag.

It is a long story.

And time is short."

I handed the prize to Esmeralda, the judge.

Rosamond clapped her hands.

"Oh, goody green grasshoppers!" she said.

"Now we can have the contest."

"Yes, I, Nate the Great,

solved the case," I said.

"But Sludge solved it first."

Esmeralda said,

"That was a very smart thing for Sludge to do.

But every pet will have a chance

to do something smart. Let's begin."

I, Nate the Great, had to watch and listen

while Oliver's eel swam backward,

Fang did something stupid with his fangs,

Rosamond's cats shed hair on command,

Finley's rat found some hidden cheese

and Pip's parrot forgot her entire speech.

Then Esmeralda said, "The winner is . .

SLUDGE!!! The only pet

who can solve a mystery."

Sludge looked proud.

I, Nate the Great, looked proud.

Everyone congratulated Sludge.

Esmeralda handed the prize to him.

Sludge sniffed it.

But he did not know

what to do with it.

He was now the owner

of a very strange tuna fish can

with smudged gold letters.

Sludge and I went home with the prize.

I gave him a huge bone.

Sludge thought it was the best prize of all.

The case was over.

But I had something left to do.

I unpacked the grocery bag,

threw away the dog shampoo

and made some pancakes.

Because I, Nate the Great,

deserved a prize, too.